My Spring Robin

By Anne Rockwell
Pictures by Harlow Rockwell & Lizzy Rockwell

Aladdin Paperbacks

For Dr. Mike Marino

First Aladdin Paperbacks edition March 1996
Text copyright © 1989 by Anne Rockwell
Illustrations copyright © 1989 by Harlow Rockwell and Lizzy Rockwell
Aladdin Paperbacks
An imprint of Simon & Schuster
Children's Publishing Division
1230 Avenue of the Americas
New York, NY 10020
Also available in a Simon & Schuster Books for Young Readers edition
The text of this book was set in 24-point Spartan Book.
The illustrations were rendered in pencil and watercolor.
Manufactured in Hong Kong
10 9 8 7 6 5
The Library of Congress has cataloged the hardcover edition as follows:
Rockwell, Anne F. My spring robin/by Anne Rockwell; pictures by
Harlow Rockwell and Lizzy Rockwell.—1st ed.   p.   cm.
Summary: Before finding the robin she is searching for, a child
discovers other interesting fauna and flora in her backyard.
ISBN 0-02-777611-5
[1. Spring—Fiction. 2. Robins—Fiction. 3. Nature—Fiction.]
I. Rockwell, Harlow, ill. II. Rockwell, Lizzy, ill. III. Title.
PZ7.R5943Mym   1989   [E]—dc19   88-13333
ISBN 0-689-80447-4 (Aladdin pbk.)

A robin sang a song for me
every day last summer.
I liked that robin.

But in the fall
my robin flew away.
My father said
it would come back
in the spring.
So when spring came,

I went looking for my spring robin.

I saw a bee
taking honey from a crocus,
but I didn't see my robin.

I looked into the yellow forsythia bush,

but my robin wasn't there.

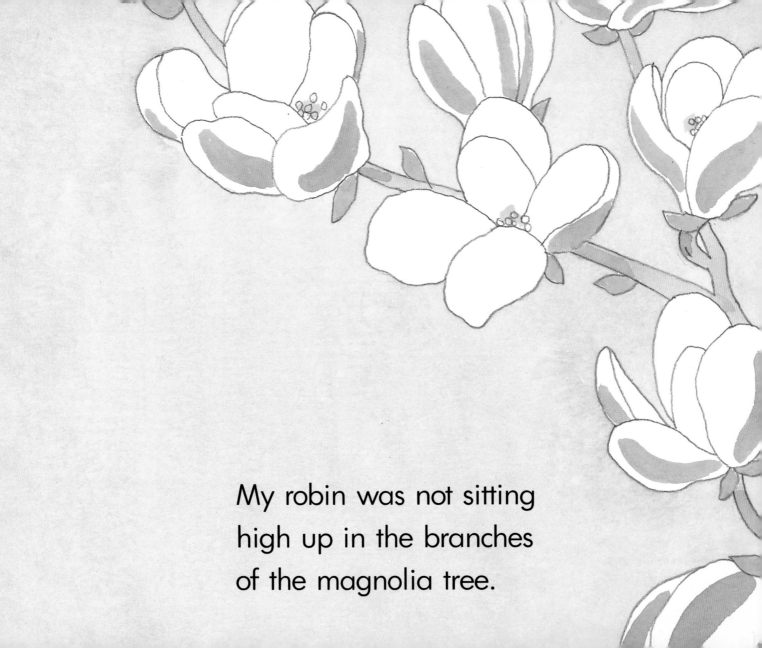

My robin was not sitting
high up in the branches
of the magnolia tree.

In the fern garden
behind our outdoor table,

fuzzy fiddleheads were sprouting
in last year's wet, brown leaves.

But I didn't see
my robin there.

I saw a tiny toad.
It hopped behind
a clump of daffodils
to hide from me.

I looked high up into the sky
to see if my robin
was flying back to me.
Drops of rain fell on my face,
and our neighbor's cat ran home.

After the shower I picked
a little bunch of purple violets
for my mother.
I watched a shiny earthworm
wriggle up out of the ground.

And then I heard it.
I heard that song!
"Cheer-up, cheerilee!
Cheer-up, cheerilee!
Cheer-up, cheerilee!"
I knew who was singing that song!

It was my spring robin!